KV-551-628

Table of Contents

Taste of Lies

I'm confused inside

I feel my soul slowly die

My brain is pulsing in

My skull

The pain is fairly dull

My thoughts are commercials

Annoying

And

Too often

Playing in my mind

BLACK

DREAMS

&

SHATTERED

ILLUSIONS

BY:

Loren Molloy

Lulu Publishing

9030 00007 1350 9

Black Dreams

And

Shattered

Illusions

By:

Loren Molloy

© 2014 Loren Molloy.
All rights reserved.
ISBN 978-1-84728-122-7

LONDON BOROUGH OF WANDSWORTH	
9030 00007 1350 9	
Askews & Holts	
JF	
	WW20001604

I know nothing

Feel everything

And I seem to be wasting my time

The tastes of lies are bitter on my tongue

The truth is too far from

Where I have begun

The lies come so easily

I have nothing solved

And

Nothing gained

Except for this pain

Lodged deep inside

My brain

Most Days

I can't get it to stop

It won't go away

Following me everywhere

Like a lost dog

It's here to stay

The pain

The hurt

The emptiness

Anger

Sadness

Lost

Regret

Most days

It sucks my energy

Like a vacuum sucks dirt

It doesn't let me sleep

It consumes my world

If you're in it

Feelings of jealousy

And

Worry

When you're not

Razors

Slit your heart

No beds of roses

No candle light dinners

No mornings after

Just you

Alone.

Boo Hoo

Today

What'd I say?

What'd I do?

Yelled at again

I don't need this shit

Not from you!

"Bite Me" I yell back

The sight of you

Makes me sick

Go pick on someone else

You friggin' Dick!

God what'd I say to make

You be like this

My body shakes

I feel my mind start to break

I play it over

And

Over

In my head

I should have just stayed

In bed!

What'd I do, breathe?

Please cut the shit

You're not that good

But one day

One day you'll get yours

Yep

Just slam that door!

What'd I do?

Oh Boo Hoo...

I'm not what you

Expected me to be

See I'm not tryin' to be you

Fuck you too!

What'd I do?

Roll my eyes?

You'd do it too if you saw you!

Askin' stupid questions again?

Been listenin' to them

Every friggin' day

I'd pay...

Just to have you

Shut up for once

I'm no dunce

I'm not going to try to make you understand

That's not my plan

You've done enough

Fucked me up for good

Should let you know

No…

You'll never know how

You've fucked me over

You've made me paranoid

You've made me crazy

Faded me into the background

Like a fuckin' daisy

What'd I do?

What'd I say today?

Boo Hoo

Hate Me…

Don't you?

AIR

My lungs crushed

Cemented like pavement

Air stopped flowing to

My brain

I've become a fish

Out of water

Must breath

Got to stay afloat

My lungs need a

Re-haul

A new model

I have a vice on my body

Squeezing my life away

Pavement for lungs

Meat grinder for brains

I've become the machinery.

Alcohol in the wound

Its venom coursing

Through my veins

Sounds like vinegar

And tastes of lemons

Sour and disgusting

Rage and depression

Looking back,

No meaning to

What I'd say

No truth in the

Harshness of my tone

Rotting meat

Soap in my mouth

Pepper on your tongue

All rage

And

Depression

Alcohol

In the wound of

Truth.

Only Words

What does it even mean?

Heathen

Bastard

Coward

Lover

Satanist

Partner

Truth

Honor

Love

All of these are

Just words

All striving for meaning

In

A world devoid

No sunrises

Only

sunsets.

Magic 8 Ball

Too many questions

Internal

And

Broad

Rhetorical

And

Unanswerable

Ever since

Wishing

For answers

Using the reliable

Magic 8 ball

Yes

Or

No

Tell me true

What should I do?

Flakes of

Thoughts

Have I made a

Romance out of a lie?

I think of you

And

I Breath a deep

Regretful sigh

We were young once

Now that's all gone

Gone

Gone

The word rings inside

Of me

Like a monks gong

Deep

And

Resounding

Shaking my body

With awareness

Have I made a

Romance out of a lie?

Out of the ashes of memories

The flakes of thoughts

Dust of moments

Imagination runs

Too wild

As flowers

Bloom

And

Weeds

Grow over

My heart

And

Soul

As a child

Naïve

And

Young

I loved you

Without

Thought

Reason

Nor

Rhythm

Now time

Ticks by

And

I think back

To you

And once again

With my deep

Regretful sigh

I cry

Why did *us* have to die?

Dread

I can't sleep

Dreams invade my mind

I can't breath

For thoughts of you

Infect me

I stare

As time winds down

'Til dawn arrives

Stories play out in my bed

Never of me

But you instead

My stomach

In knots

My throat

Filled with clenched tears

My past rots away

Inside of my memory

I'm so confused

I'm so mixed up

I might have loved you

But

Obviously

It wasn't enough

I can't do anything

About it now,

Here in bed

But

Here I sit

With

Knives of dread

How do I fix

My life?

Was it me

Or

Was it you?

Who really

Caused the doom?

Want to cry

And

I feel

Like I've died

Why didn't you want me?

Like a Song I've

Heard

You're like a song I've heard

Repeating in my soul

Losing the words

But

Still taking hold

Only remembering the melody

Days go by

And

Still you're there

Holding on

But

Without

No care

Ridiculously

Staying in

My memory

If only you were

Another song

One that doesn't end

All wrong

Filled with images

You're like a song I've heard

Sticking with me

Through my days

Running through me

Like some maze

Twists

And

Turns

No end in sight

Hope

Without

Hope

For some ray of light

This heart needs to mend

And

I want this to end

Abruptly like a song

Forgetting

For all

My days long

ALONE

Alone

Arm

Draped over your pillow

Alone

Walking the streets

Dancing at clubs

Alone

Kissing lips

Entwining arms

Still alone

In a crowded room

Contemplating death

Alone

Staring at the full moon

Loving the twinkling stars

Alone

Drinking 'til sun up

Alone

Miserable drunk

Contemplating death

Alone

Writs

Slit

Bathtub

Full

Finally

Not Alone

My Sanity

This pen

This paper

Should erase my past

It's all here

The pain,

The memories

Yet

Still

It haunts me

It can't possibly last

No matter how much

I pour onto you

Still

There is no relief

Everything is a mistake

Ones

I cannot fix

It has nothing to do

With

Perfection

Everything to do with

My sanity

This pen

This paper

My outlet

No hope

No end

No real relief

What a Trip

Purple elephants

Red tigers

Yellow penguins

Acid trips

Infuses the mind

And it wastes

Too much time

Rotting the brain

As the penguin speaks

Cantonese

The pizza is doing a dance

The walls are being tongued

Stupid Acid trips

Just are

No fun

Hendrix is speaking to me

Through the cat

'Shrooms are great

In theory

The magical show

They give

My brain

Is often

Too

Eerie

Dirt tastes

Like cake

And

I'm sure

In the morning

When I wake

All of this

Will spew

Out of me.

<u>Don't</u>

It is a world full of don'ts

Conformities

Sins on the soul

We are made to pay for

Silent as a Monk

Good as gold

Perfection on the outside

Nuns on the inside

Soon

Don't breath

Don't image.

World devoid of color

Only black and white

Jail bars

Surrounding

Your personality

Referees on your life

Penalty for unnecessary loving;

One Hundred

Tears shed

How dare I?

Sweetness punished

Only the rude survive.

Drink!

Do drugs!

Just

Don't

Be your own

Person

Empathy

Sympathy

What are they?

Rape

Murder

Give us there

Numbing effect

Why should we care?

If people

Live

Or

Die

Survive

Or

Crumble?

Conform!

Die on the

Inside

To

Survive

On the

Outside

Don't smile

Don't laugh

Don't be kind

Don't cry

These are now

Unnecessary emotions

I say...

Bah!

Hum bug!

Iron Jawed

Angels

Have things changed?

Do we need the

Iron Jawed Angels

Still?

It's called a movement

Does it still carry on?

Is there still fuel in its engine?

No more is there

One

United

Voice

The Days

And

The sentiments

Have flowed

Us down separate

Rivers.

At one time women knew

What needed to be done

Now do any of us think

For ourselves?

Once Women

had no voice

So

We mutilate that dishonorable thought

Once

Only men were heard

And

Only men were seen as human

As angels

We flew in

And

Saved our civilization

From that Molding

corruption Once we

were slaves to Any XY

chromosomes Once we

were only Good as

providers of Sex

And

Food

Prostitutes

And

Bakers, With

no thoughts

In

Our heads

Once

We wore girdles

And

Corsets,

Not only to bind our fat

But also to remind us

We are bound to them.

To remind us that

We are lower

Like a latter We

climbed Up and

over

Those rude shackles.

Time went by People

Forgot

About our

Movement,

Until once again we

Got our pride kicked,

As a jackass startled

This time it's wasn't

Our vote they wanted

To disallow

It was our choice over

Our own bodies Once

again, Politicians

forgot

We have thoughts,

A mind,

And

A power over

Ourselves.

They forgot that if

it Were them

Our XY Counterparts

Would want to make

Their own choices.

Women

Died.

People ignored

Our protests

Women Died

"Our Right, Our Choice!"

Finally

Row V. Wade

Hooray

Our Choice

Our Right

Is now not a chant of

protest But

A statement

In doctor's offices

And

In congress

Time moved on

People forgot our movements once

again People forgot the hardships

We

As women, Had

to endure People

forgot the

Women who died

So

We could have rights

The women's movement

Re-instated

Never should the thought pass through minds

Never should the

Words

Even as a Question Be

so much as uttered

"Over turn Row V. Wade"

Suddenly we are back

To the 1960's

Burning bra's in protest

Screaming chants of rage

Our Bodies

Our Choices!

Time moves forward

Or

Does it?

Are we suddenly

going To have to

protest Our Rights

Again?

Haven't enough lives been lost?

Haven't we been reduced to puddles

Under governments feet?

Enough already! If

African Americans

Can get their rights

And

Keep them

Then why

Do we have to continuously

be Slaves to politics?

Why do we have to

Incessantly fight for

The same rights

over And

Over again? We

are as equal as

Anyone but have to

Fight harder than

Anyone

Have things changed?

<u>Overjoyed</u>

I'm needed

I'm wanted

Never before has it

Been said

Those words,

Their meaning

The weight has been

Lifted

And so has

My dread

The pride

The love

The tears

The joy

The hope

Are now

Within me

Blooming

And

Blossoming

One simple statement

Years of pain

Has disappeared

Speechless

And

Blushing

Silent

And

Still

He loves me

He cares

Now

I don't feel so ill

Never

Before

It'll stay in my heart

Through

Bad

And

Worse

I won't let it part

These words

That

Healed

My

Broken

Heart.

.

Lightning Source UK Ltd.
Milton Keynes UK
UKHW030642170620
365154UK00003B/164